Cookie

by Linda Kneeland
Illustrated by Todd Fargo

JASON & NORDIC PUBLISHERS
EXTON, PENNSYLVANIA

Other Turtle Books

A Smile From Andy
Patrick and Emma Lou
Andy finds a Turtle
Danny and the Merry-Go-Round
How About a Hug

Text copyright© 1989 Linda Kneeland
Illlustrations copyright© **1989 Todd Fargo**

Library of Congress Cataloging-in-Publication Data

Kneeland, Linda, 1947 —
    Cookie / by Linda Kneeland; illustrated by Todd Fargo.
      p.   cm.
Summary: When four-year-old Molly with Down's syndrome learns to talk
with her hands, she suffers fewer frustrations by being able to ask for what
she wants.
    ISBN 0-944727-05-0
    [1. Down's syndrome — Fiction. 2. Mentally handicapped — Fiction.
З Speech — Disorders — Fiction. 4. Physically handicapped — Fiction.]
I. Fargo, Todd, 1963 —   ill.   II. Title.
PZ7.K7335Co   1989
[E] — dc20   89-35629
                                         CIP
                                         AC

ISBN 0-944727-05-0
Printed in the U.S.A.

For my dear ones — Stephanie, Katie and Chase

Also for Carolyn who was a great model!

A special thanks to the real Susan who taught us how to talk with our hands when spoken words didn't work.

Molly had a busy morning.

She had stacked blocks high into tall buildings.

She put them side-by-side into trains. She lined them into colorful designs.

Now she felt hungry.

Molly hurried to the kitchen. She tugged at the refrigerator door. Inside she saw . . . .

milk. Molly wasn't hungry for milk.
She saw cheese. Molly wasn't hungry for cheese.
She saw lettuce. Molly wasn't hungry for lettuce.
Molly was hungry for a cookie . . . a soft, chewy, chocolaty cookie. She closed the refrigerator and looked around.

The cookie jar sat high on the shelf. Molly knew there were cookies in that jar — soft, chewy chocolaty cookies.

Molly pushed the big red kitchen chair to the counter.

She climbed — first one knee up, then
the other. Molly stretched tall and thin. . .

"Molly! What are you doing up there?" Mommy asked, rushing into the kitchen. "You're going to fall off that chair and hurt yourself. Please get down."

"Do you want something to eat?"
Mommy asked.

Molly nodded. I want a soft, chewy,
chocolaty cookie, Molly thought.

"Would you like . . . a pretzel?"

Molly shook her head 'no'. Not a pretzel.

"Some raisins?" Mommy guessed again.

No. Molly frowned and shook her
head 'no' again.
"Crackers?" Mommy asked.

No, Molly thought. No, no, no, no, NO! I want a soft, chewy, chocolaty cookie.

Molly sat down on the floor and cried.

Daddy came into the kitchen and lifted Molly onto his lap. She leaned against Daddy.

"We know you want something," Daddy said, "but we don't know what it is."

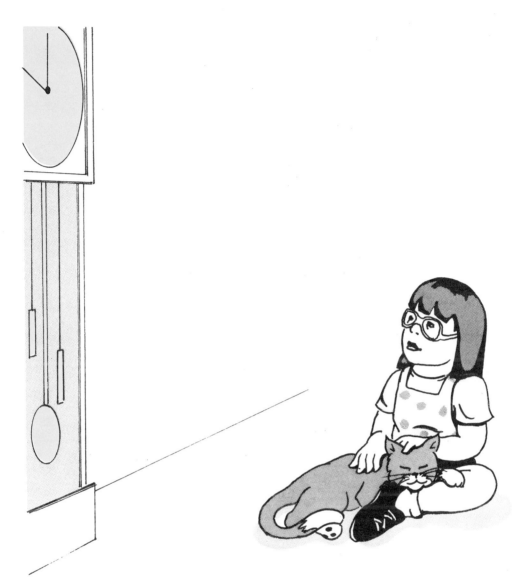

"Someone special is coming over today, Molly, someone who will help us know what to do."

You just have to wait until the clock strikes three," Daddy said. "That's when Someone Special will be here!"

Molly waited and waited. At last the clock chimed — one, two, three.

Molly looked out the window. Someone Special stood on the doorstep just as
Daddy had promised. She carried a big
bag, the biggest, lumpiest bag Molly had
ever seen.

Mommy opened the door. "Hello, Susan," Mommy said. Molly peeked out from behind the door. "Molly, this is Susan."

Susan came in, sat on the floor and opened the big bag. "Come, sit down Molly. Would you like to play with this?" Susan asked, taking something from the bag. She gave Molly a flowered pocketbook with a big plastic zipper. Inside Molly found a doll's bed, a mirror, a small yellow horse. Molly liked the doll and doll's bed best.

Soon Susan asked, "Molly, do you like cookies?" Molly opened her eyes very wide! She thought of the soft, chewy, chocolaty cookies she had tried to get earlier. Molly nodded, yes.

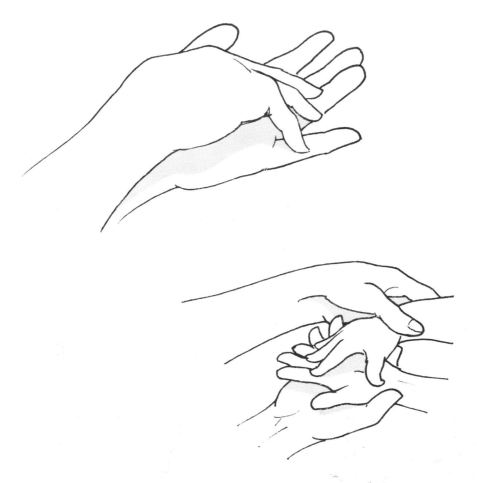

Susan held her hands out and turned the fingers of her right hand on the palm of her left hand. "Cookie," Susan said to Molly. "This is the way we say 'cookie' with our hands."

"Cookie", Susan said again as she turned Molly's hand just the way she had turned her own. "Now you're signing the word for cookie."

They all practiced it together —
Molly, Susan and Mommy.

Then Susan said, "Let's have some
juice to go with our cookies."

Susan, Molly and Mommy all signed 'juice'. Molly sipped her juice and thought, this is the best juice I've ever tasted!

Molly felt sad when it was time for Susan to leave. "Good-bye, now, Molly. I'll come back another time and we can sign some new words," Susan said. Molly blew Susan a kiss.

Mommy closed the door and said, "We've had a busy afternoon, Miss Molly, now we must start dinner." Molly watched Susan drive out of sight.

"Would you come and help set the table?" Mommy called.

Dinner, thought Molly. Suddenly, she felt very, very hungry.

She raced into the kitchen and saw Mommy putting placemats on the table.

Molly took the napkins and carefully
put one beside each plate. She smoothed
the last napkin.

Suddenly she had a great idea!

Molly held her hands out. She put one hand on top of the other, turning it in a circle just as Susan had showed her. She looked at Mommy.

Would it work? Would Mommy know what she wanted this time?

Mommy looked at Molly. Molly made
the sign again — one hand on the other
and turn.

"Why Molly! That's the sign for 'cookie'! Do you want a cookie?"

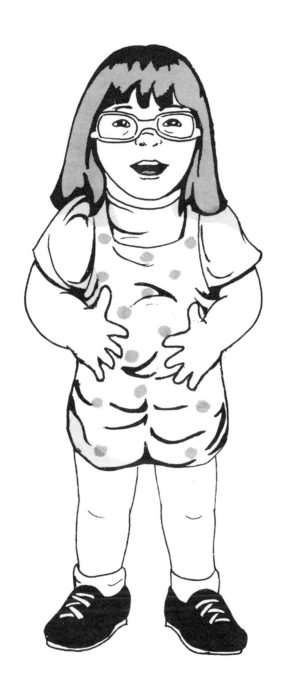

Molly clapped her hands together
happily and nodded 'yes'.

"I'm so proud of you," Mommy said, giving Molly a big hug and kiss. "That was so wonderful . . . let's ALL have cookies tonight! I'll get the plate . . . you can put the cookies on it."

Molly put a huge pile of soft, chewy,
chocolaty chocolate chip cookies on the
plate. . .

AND took the biggest one for herself.
Molly felt happy all over.

Can you make the sign for 'cookie'?

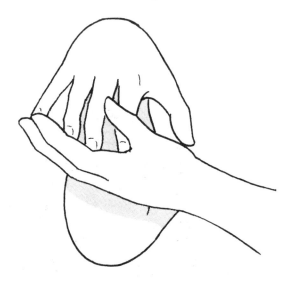

Can you make the sign for 'juice'?

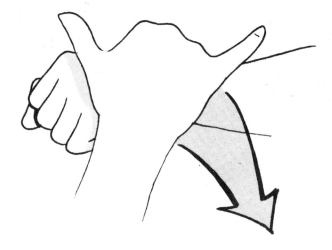

That's right! Good job!